the first part last

the first part last

ANGELA JOHNSON

Simon & Schuster Books for Young Readers
New York London Toronto Sydney Singapore

SIMON & SCHUSTER
BOOKS FOR YOUNG READERS
An imprint of Simon & Schuster
Children's Publishing Division
1230 Avenue of the Americas
New York, NY 10020

SIMON & SCHUSTER BOOKS FOR YOUNG READERS
is a trademark of Simon & Schuster.

Book design by O'Lanso Gabbidon

The text for this book is sent in Aldine401.
Printed in the United States of America

8 10 9 7

Library of Congress Cataloging-in-Publication Data
Johnson, Angela.
The first part last / by Angela Johnson
p. cm.
Summary: Bobby's carefree teenage life changes forever
when he becomes a father and must care for his adored
baby daughter.
ISBN 0-689-84922-2
[1. Teenage fathers—Fiction. 2. Teenage parents—Fiction.
3. Father and child—Fiction. 4. Babies—Fiction. 5. African
Americans—Fiction.] I. Title.
PZ7.J629 Fi 2003
[Fic]—dc21
2002036512

*For Elizabeth Acevedo
and the rest of the students
in the 1999–2000 sixth-grade class
at the Manhattan School for Children*

the first part last

part
I

now

MY MOM SAYS that I didn't sleep through the night until I was eight years old. It didn't make any difference to her 'cause she was up too, listening to the city. She says she used to come into my room, sit cross-legged on the floor by my bed, and play with my Game Boy in the dark.

We never talked.

I guess I thought she needed to be there. And she must have thought her being there made everything all better for me.

Yeah.

I get it now. I really get it.

We didn't need to say it. We didn't have to look at each other or even let the other one know we saw each other in the glow of the Game Boy.

So last week when it looked like Feather probably wasn't ever going to sleep through the night, I lay her on my stomach and breathed her in. My daughter is eleven days old.

And that sweet new baby smell . . . the smell of baby shampoo, formula, and my mom's perfume. It made me cry like I hadn't since I was a little kid.

It scared the hell out of me. Then, when Feather moved on my stomach like one of those mechanical dolls in the store windows at Christmas, the tears dried up. Like that.

I thought about laying her in the middle of my bed and going off to find my old Game Boy, but I didn't.

Things have to change.

I've been thinking about it. Everything. And when Feather opens her eyes and looks up at me, I already know there's change. But I figure if the world were really right, humans would live life backward and do the first part last. They'd be all knowing in the beginning and innocent in the end.

Then everybody could end their life on their momma or daddy's stomach in a warm room, waiting for the soft morning light.

then

AND THIS IS how I turned sixteen. . . .

Skipped school with my running buddies, K-Boy and J. L., and went to Mineo's for a couple of slices. Hit a matinee and threw as much popcorn at each other as we ate. Then went to the top of the Empire State Building 'cause I never had before.

I said what everybody who'd ever been up there says.

"Everybody looks like ants."

Yeah, right. . . .

Later on that night my pops, Fred, made my favorite meal—cheese fries and ribs—at his restaurant. I caught the subway home and walked real slow 'cause I knew my mom had a big-ass cake for me when I got there, and I was still full. (In my family, special days mean nonstop food.)

I never had any cake though 'cause my girl-friend Nia was waiting on our stoop for me with a red balloon. Just sittin' there with a balloon, looking all lost. I'll never forget that look and how her voice shook when she said, "Bobby, I've got something to tell you."

Then she handed me the balloon.

now

I USED TO LAUGH when this old dude, "Just Frank" from the corner, used to ask me if I was being a "man." He never seemed to ask anybody else if they were being men; at least I never heard him. I laughed 'cause I didn't consider him much of one, a man, hangin' on the corner, drinking forties at ten in the morning. Hell, he was a joke. Always had been.

Two days after I brought Feather home, Just Frank got killed trying to save a girl in the neighborhood from being dragged into an alley by some nut job.

Didn't have any family. Didn't have any money, Just Frank. So the block got together to pay for his funeral, or the city was going to bury him in Potter's

Field. I went to his funeral at Zion AME, then walked home and held Feather for the rest of the night, wondering if I would be a man, a good man.

Feather sleeps like these kittens I saw once at a farm my summer camp went to. They were all curled up in an old crate, sleeping with paws on their brothers and sisters. Sleeping safe and with family.

I haven't been able to put her in her own bed at night, which used to be mine, since she came home from the hospital.

Mary, my mom, says I'm going to pay.

"Put that baby down, Bobby. I swear she's going to think the whole world is your face. She's going to be scared out of her mind when she turns about six and you haven't put her down long enough to see any of it."

Or . . .

"Bobby, you could have let your Aunt Victoria hold the baby for more than the thirty seconds it took for you to go to the bathroom. You are going to pay when she starts walking and won't let you out of her sight. You'll pay."

I wonder if somebody threatened her that one day I'd love her and want to be with her all the time. Some threat.

• • •

K-Boy and J. L. stand over Feather's bed, making faces and loud noises at her.

She screams.

They shake a rattle at her and tickle her feet.

She screams again.

I dive across my bed and put my Walkman on and watch them, laughing. "Yeah, you two are real good with her. If I was a baby I'd stop crying if a couple of tall men made scary faces at me and shook loud rattling sticks at my head."

J. L. picks her up like she's a football and walks her to the bedroom window. "Hey, man, my sister's got a baby, and I always get him to stop crying."

He starts to rock back and forth on his heels, humming something that I really can't hear. After about a minute she's stopped crying, and J. L. has slid to the floor with her. He keeps on humming. I see Feather's hands slowly rise then relax, and I know she's finally asleep. And in a few minutes J. L. is too.

K-Boy is standing at my desk, running his hand over a drawing that I did of Feather last night. "Nice."

"Thanks."

K-Boy takes his baseball cap off and his locks

fall all over his face. He's mahogany and tall, and can't walk down the street without everybody staring at him. He's beautiful, but acts like he doesn't know it (Mom says). When we were ten he was almost six feet tall, and people who didn't know him treated him older. It would piss him off, people expecting teenage stuff from him when we were still jumping off swings at the playground.

K-Boy doesn't date. He just hangs out with girls. When I say stuff like this can happen to anybody (meaning a baby), even if you are just kicking it with some girl, K-Boy says no. It's different.

Everything is different if there ain't no love.

Didn't want to hear that then. And I guess I don't really want to hear it now. He's one of my best friends, but he's always saying stuff that makes me crazy.

Worse even is when he doesn't say anything at all. Then I got to wonder.

He keeps looking at the drawing of Feather.

"So. You going to keep her or what?"

I turn down my Walkman and look at him for a long time, wondering why he's my friend. "What do you mean am I going to keep her?"

He sits down on the bed beside me and grabs

the TV remote and starts watching a gardening show, muted. "It's a question, man."

"It's a stupid fucking question, K."

"Naw, Bobby, it's just a question. What's the problem?"

"Ain't no problem. No problem," I almost scream. Feather jumps in J. L.'s arms and his eyes snap open.

J. L. yawns. "What up?"

Nobody says anything. K-Boy turns the volume up on the TV, and I turn the volume up on my Walkman. J. L. nods off again.

A few minutes later this woman on TV is pointing at a mountain of dirt, and I say—like I'm talking to myself—"No doubt in my mind that I'm keeping her."

A few minutes after that, K-Boy has turned to the Weather Channel, but is looking across the room at J. L. and Feather. He says, "Too right you should keep her, man, too right."

then

FRED AND MARY SAT REAL STILL, and for a while I thought what I just told them about Nia being pregnant had turned both of them to stone.

It had been a long time since either of them ever agreed on anything.

So I waited. I waited to hear how they'd been talking to me for years about this. How we all talked about respect and responsibility. How Fred and me had taken the ferry out to Staten Island and talked about sex, to *and* from the island. And didn't we go together and get me condoms? What the hell about those pamphlets Mary put beside my bed about STDs and teenage pregnancy?

How did this happen? Where was my head? Where was my sense? What the hell were we going to do?

And then, not moving and still quiet, my pops just starts to cry.

now

MY BONES ACHE TIRED, but I'm wide awake.

I must be the only person up now. Even the city is quiet. Our neighborhood at least. I don't know what that means, except everyone in the world must have a new baby who kept them up most of the night and they've all passed out.

The rules.

>*If she hollers, she is mine.*
>*If she needs to be changed, she is always mine.*
>*In the dictionary next to "sitter," there is not a picture of Grandma.*
>*It's time to grow up.*
>*Too late, you're out of time. Be a grown-up.*

• • •

I can hear Mary turn over in her sleep in the next room. She doesn't wake up 'cause Feather hasn't screamed yet. She whimpered herself awake, which means she only wants to be put in the bed beside me. No diaper change or formula needed. No big screaming fit. She only wants Daddy.

That scares the sh

Just me.

This little thing hands doing nothing but counting on me. And me wanting nothing else but to run crying into my own mom's room and have her do the whole thing.

It's not going to happen, and my heart aches as I straighten out her hands and trace the delicate lines. Then kiss them. Her hands are translucent and warm. Baby hands. Warm, sweet-smelling baby hands. And all I can do is kiss them and pull her closer so she won't see my face and how scared I am.

When there's nothing you can do, do nothing.

But then I realize. I've done it. I know something. I know something about this little thing that is my baby. I know that she needs me. I know what she does when she just needs me.

No big screaming thing.
Just a whimper, then she only wants me.

Eight extra diapers.
Baby corn starch.
Baby wipes.
Three binkies (in case two get lost).
Four six-ounce bottles.
Three Onesies.
Three changes of outfits (she's barfing a lot).
One change of booties.
Diaper rash ointment.
Non-aspirin baby drops.
Two rattles.
One extra beanie.
Two cans of soy formula.
One can opener.
Two bottles of spring water.
And one cell phone all fit into the diaper bag K-Boy's mom gave to me two days after Feather was born. It all fits. Everything I need to get me from the Upper West Side to Bed Stuy for a whole day with Grandpa.

A few trains later and a nap (the motion just about puts me out right along with Feather) gets me to Pops.

When we get buzzed in and I'm holding her in

the carrier, going up in the 'vator, I think about the first time I came here, hand in hand with Fred, after him and Mary separated. I have to lean against the sides 'cause I could break down any minute. Just fall apart anytime before I get to my pop's apartment, which probably smells like chili-cheese fries. Just for me.

then

THEY ALWAYS LIKED ME.

Nia's parents always treated me good and trusted me. She told me they did. I didn't think much about it the whole time me and Nia used to be with each other.

I didn't think about it when we were on the subway to school, or hanging out at Mineo's, or skating in the park. What was I supposed to think about it, except it just was. It's good to be trusted, but you take it as it is. Nothing more. Nothing less.

Every wall in their loft is so white it almost hurts my eyes. Everything is straight lines and post-modern sculpture backlit. Stark white and so neat and clean you could probably make soup in the toilet.

I used to love this house 'cause I grew up in a place so different.

We have overstuffed pillows and Moroccan rugs and Jacob Lawrence prints all over the walls. Color and sound is what my parents were always about. Me and my brothers grew up in a loud house with jazz, Motown, or reggae music always playing in the background and something always on the stove.

Black-and-white pictures of my brothers and me in Africa, Spain, and Venezuela and Malaysia sit on every table, shelf, or furniture surface there is in the whole place. 'Cause even though Fred said we were poor, we never were too poor to travel, 'cause that made your spirit rich. He said.

To me, our house was crowded and noisy.

Nia lived in space and quiet.

When she comes through the Japanese doors that separate the bedrooms from the rest of the loft, Nia is backlit too. Just like a sculpture.

I see her like I never saw anybody before. Bathed in light like one of those angels in the paintings at the museums. So when she comes and sits by me, I almost holler when her hand covers mine and her silver and cowrie bracelet brushes against me.

She says, "They're coming in a minute. My

dad's on the phone and my mom . . ." She doesn't have to say anything else 'cause in a second her mom's backlit too, beside her father, and all I want to do is to get out of the light, back to the soft edges and color with something cooking on the stove.

They're cool and calm and sit hand in hand on the white couch with iron arms.

She smiles, her hair pulled back from her round face. I can just make out the circles under her eyes that she's covered with makeup.

He looks straight ahead like he's watching a movie outside the loft windows. It's like nothing that is about to be said or happen has that much to do with him.

He reminds me of my uncle L. C. when anybody starts talking about my cousin Sam who quit law school and went to be an aid worker in Africa. He just looks straight ahead and talks about the weather.

Oh, hell is all I can think when I know it's my turn to talk.

Yeah, Mr. Wilkins, I got your daughter pregnant.

Yeah, Mrs. Wilkins, I know that this is a tragedy 'cause you all expected more responsible behavior from us.

Oh, hell yeah, we know what's in store for us.

I can't tell you how upset my parents are, and the way my dad cried, and the way my mom wanted to slap me so hard she bit her lip till it bled down her chin.

No. I don't have any plans except shooting hoops with my partners at the rec center, and hanging out till we get bored and take in a movie. (Is this what you meant, Mr. Wilkins? Is this what you wanted me to say instead of I'm going to be the best father to me and Nia's baby that there ever was?)

But I say,

Yes, sir.

Yes, ma'am.

I don't know, ma'am.

I know, sir.

And on and on till it's like I'm almost blind from the cool white walls and the smile that hasn't left Nia's mom's face. 'Cause I know Nia told me she only does that when she's pissed and can't deal.

Then I know it's over when they both stand up and say something about wanting to speak to my parents, and Nia starts crying. I hate it that she cries first, before I do.

now

I HOLD MY BABY in a waiting room that I used to sit in, way before I had her.

The nurse is the same one that has been smiling at me since my mom used to carry me in on her hip. The corkboard by the water fountain is still filled with pictures of kids, most laughing. The play area still has beat-up stuffed animals and cans of crayons pushed up against building blocks, dolls, and trucks.

I remember sitting here with Mary when I had a fever, needed to get stitches out, had to get a booster shot, fell into some poison ivy on vacation, and about a thousand other things that my pediatrician, Dr. Victor, took care of.

Now I'm sharing her with my daughter 'cause

I can still technically have a kid doctor for myself, even if I'm now technically a parent.

It's whacked, I know. And it didn't help that yesterday something happened that kind of messed me up.

I forgot Feather, and left her all alone.

K-Boy called me up to hit the nets a little and I said yeah. So I grabbed my basketball, zipped up my jacket, and headed out the front door.

Got all the way down the elevator.

I got all the way to the street door.

Then I was almost at the corner. . . .

She was still asleep as I crawled across the floor to her crib. Breathing that baby breath. Dreaming with baby eyes closed and sweet. And if she was older, just a little bit older, trusting that I'd be here for her.

I lay my basketball down and it rolled out the door into the hall toward Mary's room.

And I'd almost got all the way to the corner.

Dr. Victor picks Feather up and puts her on the baby scales. It's the first time I've seen her being weighed. She's a digital seven pounds and fifteen ounces.

"She's picking up weight, Bobby."

"Yeah, she drinks anything that you put in

front of her. I mean, she's doing good."

"She looks fantastic. And how are you? Tired?"

I adjust Feather's booties. Our downstairs neighbor, Coco Fernandez (I've always called her by her full name), made them out of angora (whatever that is). They're soft on the baby's feet.

Then Feather stretches and yawns like she'll never close her mouth.

I smile at Dr. Victor.

Damn, do I look tired? I want to say. Does it look like I've been up for three straight weeks with no breaks in between? I don't say it though. I just smile and try to keep from curling up in the baby carrier with the kid.

Won't do any good to complain about being tired. I already tried that with my mom. She couldn't have rolled her eyes any more than she did when I mentioned how tired I was and how maybe I wanted to go hang out awhile at the arcade.

"Your arcade days are over, brother." She laughed before she walked out the front door, mumbling something about going to develop some prints.

I smile up at Dr. Victor again. "I'm okay."

She looks at me for a minute then walks closer

and feels my neck. "I think you have swollen glands. Have you been feeling under the weather?"

I say again, "I'm okay."

Then I want to beg her for a note like I used to when I didn't want to do something and a sore knee or fever could get me out of it.

I want to say to this woman who'd always been nice to me and listened when I complained that damn it, I didn't feel good, I was so tired, I didn't know where I was going to lay down in a few hours, and by the way could she just write me a note and get me out of this?

It didn't have to be a long note.

It didn't have to tell anything about a medical condition.

It just had to get me out of staying awake all night, changing diapers every hour, and doing nothing except think of the yawning little thing in the white booties, whose baby carrier was all I wanted to be in.

I just want a note to get me out of it.

Just one note.

then

I SIT WITH NIA in a waiting room, with posters of pregnant women plastered everywhere. At least it seems like they're everywhere.

The Health Channel is starting to get on my nerves, talking about folic acid and good prenatal care, which is what we're here for. Damn, TV is everywhere. You can't even get away from it at the doctor's office. And I never thought I'd ever say that.

Nia's got her face in a magazine and hasn't looked up from it since she finished filling out the two-page questionnaire the nurse gave her.

I know she's trying to pretend she's not here.

Trying to pretend it never happened.

Trying to pretend we're just on some field trip

to the obstetrician's office. I know I'm doing a good job of denying just about everything that's been going on, to myself, so I figure she probably is too.

When I told Nia I wanted to go to her first appointment, she asked, "Why do you want to go?"

I said, "Shouldn't I go with you the first time?"

Nia starts reading her English book and not looking at me. "You don't have to, Bobby. I mean, I know how to get there by myself."

"Yeah, I know you know directions, Nia—I'm just trying to do the right thing. Mary says . . ."

Then it's the first time I see Nia really mad. It's like she wants to throw me across the room.

"So this isn't about what you really want to do. This is all about what your mom thinks you ought to do."

I try to explain, but she waves me off and walks out of study hall, and I don't have time to tell her all Mary said was that Nia's doctor was around the corner from where she had a shoot and maybe we could have lunch afterward.

Hell, I knew it wasn't going to be easy. Nothing ever is, anymore.

• • •

I don't remember everything. Just sitting in the doctor's office and looking at her skiing trophies on the shelves behind her.

I think she talked about how this whole thing should be a partnership and how Nia was going to count on me. She talked about Lamaze.

Nia said, "Uh, no. I *do* believe that all the pain medication in the world has to be used for this baby. I'm not into learning how to breathe. I do that just fine."

Then I stupidly say, "Maybe Lamaze would be better for the baby."

Nia stands up with one hand on her hip. She still only weighs about ninety pounds and isn't showing at all. But that doesn't mean she isn't full of attitude.

"Are you having this damned baby, Bobby?"

"No. Not even if I wanted to do it and spare you."

Nia chills and sits back down, grabbing my hand real tight before she looks at me with tears running down her face.

I look at the skiing trophies and think about how cool and windy it must be to go down the slopes, and how I always wanted to learn how to ski.

The doctor, I can't remember her name, says

something in a calm voice to Nia and doesn't look at me for the rest of the time we're there.

Nia keeps tapping her foot, and the doctor finally says that she needs to take Nia's blood pressure and get her ready for her exam.

"I don't have to be in there, do I?" I ask.

The doctor smiles like she feels bad for me, but not bad enough to leave the exam stuff out. But it turns out I'm wrong, because she sends me back to the waiting room to hang out till Nia is finished.

There I sit and listen to the health channel and dream that I have just sailed into the wind on skis, way into the wind, out of reach.

now

THIS MUST BE IT.

This must be what made my mom's eyes narrow and nasty words come out of her mouth.

This must be what helped give my dad an ulcer and that look on his face that says—what next?

This must be it. The place where you really feel that it's all on you and you got a kid.

Feather spent last night in the hospital, with me sitting next to her bed all night long. I've had about twenty minutes' sleep in the last three days. Almost got locked in the toilet off the waiting room 'cause I was so sleepy I hallucinated being on the subway.

I got into a fight with a nurse.

Left my backpack in the taxi I came to the hospital in.

And before all of that, Feather threw up on the last clean jacket I had, and my mom is out of town and not answering her voice mail.

Half of Pop's kitchen staff called off and he's up to his ass . . .

She's sleeping now.

They say it was just a twenty-four-hour bug, but it scared the hell out of me when I went in to get her up from her nap and she was burning up. I could feel it through her bunny-rabbit sleeper, and it totally freaked me out. When I put the thermometer cone in her ear a few seconds later, it read 104.

It's twenty-four hours later, and we're home after hospital hell. I'm trying to get some sleep, but I'm too tired, if that makes sense.

Mom finally calls. "You okay, kid?"

She already knows Feather is okay. I'd been leaving voice mails every hour. I feel like a big old baby, but I can't help it, and when I finally hear her voice . . . I start crying like one. Only quiet so she won't know.

I manage a "Umm huh," and wish she'd hurry

up and finish shooting fruit and vegetables at farm markets and get the hell back to the city.

"I'll be back tomorrow," she says.

Then some leftover idiot that lives in me says, "Take your time. We're both just hangin' out now."

"Umm huh, Bobby. Remember to get Coco if you need anything."

I don't say what I want, which is for her to get home before I get an ulcer or start cussing strangers.

Instead, I wrap Feather up tight, lock the door behind me, and thirty seconds later I'm down the iron fire stairs and at Coco's door.

"Come in if you're good looking," she yells. Then, "Come in even if you're not. I'll give you a makeover."

I walk into a powder blue apartment with squishy dark blue carpet, and pictures of her kids and grandkids everywhere. Bluegrass is playing on the stereo.

Coco is a fiddle player in a bluegrass band.

She's known me forever, and comes over and starts kissing Feather before she takes her out of my arms.

"I got your message," she says, smiling so her whole face scrunches up. She's got some sort of twenty-colored scarf tying all her dark hair up, and she's wearing one of her hundred "I Luv NY" shirts with sweatpants. I've been taller than her my whole life, and Feather probably weighs more than her. They are the same caramel color, though.

"I figured I'd missed you." I yawn.

"Yeah. We had a gig at this revival in the Village. I hadn't seen a lot of those people since the seventies."

I sit down and watch the fish in Coco's aquarium swim back and forth.

The next thing I know, it's six hours later and Feather is asleep beside me on Coco's couch.

I've got about three hours before school starts.

Feather wakes up as I carry her up the fire stairs and unlock the door to our apartment.

When I walk past my mom's room, I miss her.

I walk to my room, put Feather in her crib, which pisses her off and makes her scream, and then I look around my room and miss me.

then

K-Boy and J. L. lean against the wall of the West Side Rec Center and don't say anything. Then they shift their stance and look across the street while three girls cross it, talking loud and laughing. And when the girls almost get hit by a taxi, they flip the driver off and keep on walking.

J. L. laughs and sucks down the bottle of water he pulled out of his backpack a minute ago.

I keep waiting.

I keep waiting for them to say anything about what I just told them. For the first time I don't know what they'll say. I know it's stupid, but I'm more afraid of what they'll say about Nia being pregnant than I was about my parents.

J. L. is the first to open his mouth.

"Yo, Bobby. I need some money for a phone call. You got change on you?"

And I'm thinking, I just told him my girl is having a baby and all he wants to do is make a phone call.

I reach into my pocket and K-Boy starts laughing.

"What the hell is so funny?" I yell at him 'cause both of them are seriously starting to get on my nerves. What the hell, anyway?

K-Boy stops laughing, but he really doesn't want to.

J. L. leans back against the Center again. "Hey, Bro, I was just going to make a call for you to 1-800-ISTUPID."

K-Boy looks sorry for me and starts shaking his head. I don't know what I expected. I would have probably said the same thing.

We all talked about this. We said only stupid people would let it get to this. 'Cause there is birth control. Lots of it.

My mom always kept a big basket of rubbers underneath the bathroom sink for my brothers, and when they both left—just me. She said she didn't want to have to talk about it every time she thought about it.

So there they were.

K-Boy and J. L. got most of their supplies from me,

J. L. 'cause he was always broke and K-Boy 'cause his moms almost lost her mind when she found a pack of condoms underneath his bed.

She didn't want to hear he was being safe. She just wanted him not to do it. Didn't want to ever know that he thought about sex, had sex, or hung out with people who might be having sex too.

"What can I say?" K-Boy shrugged.

"What do you want us to say?" J. L. said, looking kind of sorry he'd been an asshole a few minutes ago.

"Nothing," I say, and turn to watch the little kids running around the rec center playground. And I'm thinking while I'm watching how in three or four years my kid's going to be out there screaming and falling down with the rest of them.

J. L. picks his backpack off the ground and starts walking off. He doesn't turn around for almost a block. When he finally does, K-Boy nods to him, and I act like I don't even see him.

"Shit. Never seen J. L. like that," K-Boy says.

We start walking down Columbus and I don't hear the people or cars, and it's rush hour. Everything is a blur, and the only thing I see is my feet in hiking boots and K-Boy in tennis shoes.

K-Boy says, "Shit," again.

"Yeah," I say. "That's pretty much where I'm at."

K-Boy brushes against my shoulder trying to dodge two kids on Rollerblades.

"Nia okay? 'Cause I know she is seriously into the books. . . ."

"She's out of it. Last time I talked to her all she could do is get out a few words. Mostly she just cries."

"I feel you, man. I mean I wouldn't want to be ya, but I feel you."

"Hell, I don't want to be me either."

Two girls pass by us and stare at K-Boy. I mean they stop in the middle of the sidewalk and stare. He smiles back.

I grab him by the arm. "Uh huh, they are so fine, but not today."

K-Boy laughs, looks at me, and we keep on walking.

"So—she keeping it or what?"

I say, "I don't know. She doesn't want to talk about it. She doesn't say yes. She doesn't say no."

"Bobby, what do you want her to do?"

My stomach is hurting by the time that question is out of his mouth and into the air. I don't say; it's not up to me. I don't say; whatever I want, I can't say. My dad already told me now was the time to shut my mouth. What Nia wants is what it's all about.

No pressure.

A minute later I'm puking in front of a flower shop and K-Boy is telling the owner to stop screaming at me, grow a heart, and get out of my face.

"Shit," I say.

K-Boy takes a T-shirt out of his backpack so I can wipe off my jacket. We walk on and K doesn't stop at his turnoff, but walks me the five blocks to my apartment, watches me go in, then turns and heads home.

I sit on the stairs to catch my breath before I climb up to my floor.

now

I CAN HARDLY KEEP MY EYES OPEN in Brit Lit. I got so much drool on my arm I can't even try to wipe it on my shirt. I seriously need a tissue or a paper towel.

I was up all night with Feather, who thinks two in the morning is party time. She just smiles, though, unless you try to put her down, then she screams like it's the end of the world.

I walked her.

I played music for her. She likes dance music and can't stand the Bach for Babies my aunt bought her.

When the music stopped she screamed or twisted herself up in a bunch so tight it even made me feel cranky. So I talked to her. Told her about what was going on.

It's cool when I talk to her. I could be saying anything. I could be talking about basketball or my bad grades in math.

I could be telling her how she looks like her mom. And asking if she remembers her. It hasn't been that long ago.

As long as my mouth is moving, she's happy. As long as sound is coming out of it, the whole world is just fine for my caramel, sweet-faced, big-eyed baby; who's killing me, and keeping me so tired I can't keep my eyes open.

So in the end I'm busted by Mr. Philips, my Brit Lit teacher.

When the bell rings, he points to me and mouths, "Stay put."

I do.

And this is how it goes.

"I hear you're a father."

I rub the sleep out of my eyes, and for the first time, really the first time, notice that he's one of the tallest men I've ever met. What made him want to be a teacher? Hell, he was taller than most pro basketball players.

Why was he here? Teaching kids like me and kids who weren't like me but must be just as bad?

I keep rubbing my eyes 'cause it keeps me from having to talk. At least it seems that way to me. I'm sick of talking. I've been talking to a baby all night long and into the morning.

I notice his khakis and then his blue polo shirt. Then I look at the way the light bounces off his almost bald head. His head isn't shiny though 'cause he's got hair growing in. Maybe he's growing it back.

Hell. Why do I care? I think I might be going crazy from lack of sleep.

"I said, I heard you're a father."

Then I wake up. "Yeah, I got a baby."

"The mother go to this school?"

"She used to," I say.

He smiles like one of the social workers I had to talk to.

"Did she transfer to another school?"

I look at his shoes. Loafers. What's that about anyway?

"No."

"She helping you out? I mean, I heard that the baby is living with you."

I try the eye rubbing thing again and think how I'm going to get him out of my business. Shit! People in this school talk too much. Everybody's always got so much to say, and never really says anything that's worth talking about.

He probably drives a Jeep, and his girlfriend and him have been engaged for two years. They probably laugh at the same jokes and plan to have two kids and go to Disney in the summer.

What the hell does he know?

"Yeah, my kid lives with me."

"Well, I hope you're getting help."

Then he just leaves.

I'm thinking he's going to tell me how he'll give me a break on my grades or something. Something. But that ain't happening.

He just hopes I'm getting help.

I rub my eyes again and hope my shirt dries from all the spit on it and remember I have to stop by the store on the way home from school to pick up some more formula.

I have to change twice on the subway to get to the baby-sitter in Brooklyn to pick up Feather.

Jackie's poodle keeps barking at me. The stupid dog's known me for years and still keeps acting like it's never seen me.

What's the problem?

I walk into the toy-covered living room and remember playing in it when I was little. Nothing's changed. Nothing.

I can almost taste the toasted cheese sand-wiches and tomato soup that I couldn't get enough of.

I remember the box of play clothes and the corner off the dining room where me and Paco Morales painted the carpet polka-dot.

Jackie looks the same.

Laughs the same, shaking when she laughs and tossing her beaded braids in back of her when she puts her hands on her hips to tell one of the parents that she needs to give her baby more green vegetables to make him regular.

She's probably talked the same way to parents for thirty years.

She probably talked to my own mom that way. Everybody listened.

So when she says, "Boy, you look old and tired," I sit on the floor like I used to and think about how easy it was when me and Paco thought the carpet needed spots. She puts Feather in my arms and leans down close to me, braids clicking with beads, and says, "But it'll change for sure. I know it will. I just know."

I want to ask her how she knows, but I'm too tired, so all I can do is hold my baby and think about the two changes we have to make to get home.

then

NIA'S SCARFING DOWN TACOS like she hasn't eaten in a week. I know she ate two hours ago, because I was the one that picked up the pineapple-and-pepperoni pizza for her at Mineo's.

"It'll be cold by the time I get it to you," I said, screaming over the sound of jackhammers and taxis blowing down Broadway.

"That's okay. What do you think stoves are for? I don't mind cooking it a few more minutes."

"You sure you want a slice this early in the morning? I don't even know if they fire the oven up this early."

"Bobby, it's a pizza shop."

"Yeah, but this early they usually only serve pastries and espresso."

I'm not gonna get out of this. She wants a pizza at ten o'clock on a Saturday morning, and the quiet on the other end of the phone means she's as serious as a heart attack.

I head toward Mineo's.

And all I'm wishing is that Nia's parents didn't live in Chelsea 'cause if she was gonna get a jones for Mineo's on the Upper West Side I was going to be hopping a lot of buses.

Now she's sitting on the floor against the dining room wall, stuffing more tacos down her throat. She looks tired. And she looks good.

Real good.

She's all in black. V-neck sweater, black pants, and some sort of ruffle black thing that pulls her curly brown hair up in a ponytail.

When she takes a breather from eating, she brings her feet up, sits cross-legged, and plays with a silver toe ring on her left foot. She smiles at me sitting across from her with my back against the couch.

I say, "Feel better now?"

She nods her head, crawls across all the taco papers and salsa containers, and curls up around me. She smells like baby shampoo and hot sauce.

In a few minutes we're wrapped around each

other on the floor. She smells sweet and her mouth is tangy, then sweet, then tangy again.

All I can think is that I want her more than anything. I want her more than I've ever wanted anything, ever.

She pulls my T-shirt over my head and kisses me so soft on my neck. She's everything that I ever thought I wanted when I take her sweater off and kiss all the soft places, the warm places, down to her stomach. . . .

I stay there for a long time, warming my face on her swollen belly. She sighs and holds my head. I close my eyes and want to stay there.

"Is it too early for the baby to move?"

She giggles. "Yeah, I think so."

I look over at all the taco wrappers and the pizza box.

"I guess it's not too early for it to eat like a starving pig though."

She giggles again.

Kissing her belly is like eating ice cream. I can't stop. I don't want to stop. So I don't.

She starts to shiver and I watch her arms and stomach get goose bumps on them, so I wrap myself tighter around her.

I whisper, "Is it okay? I mean, will it hurt the baby if we do it?"

She sits up against the couch and smiles.

"No. I got all these pamphlets and things from the doctor. All of them say it's okay, just use common sense."

I figure we hadn't used too much common sense lately, or she wouldn't be pregnant.

"My parents won't be home until tonight. We've got a long time."

I pull her to me then lift her up off the floor.

We step on the pizza box as we head toward her room. I'm glad we have a long time. I'm glad.

now

I SHOULD HAVE SCOPED how the day was going when Feather puked on me just as I picked her up out of her crib this morning.

But I didn't hear it or see it.

Fred always talks about the signs being there. He says he can tell in the morning if a waiter is going to quit or some delivery isn't going to come. The only way to change something is to pay attention to the signs.

But K-Boy says it doesn't matter what you do, what's gonna go down is already set. Try to change something—be damned. Don't try to change it—be damned just as much.

So I should have just called in sick to school

and watched the purple dinosaur all day long with the baby.

I should have just hid.

But in the end there was probably nothing I could do about anything anyway. If you look at it that way I guess it makes what goes down, go down easier.

And 'cause I was going to be late getting Feather to the sitter, I knocked on Coco's door.

'Cause I had to give Feather a bath it made everything late. I'd already been called into the guidance counselor's office twice.

She smiled a lot and asked if everything was running smooth. Was fatherhood what I thought it would be? Was the responsibility of a baby getting to be too much? Was my mother helping? My father? The baby's other grandparents?

I fell asleep in her warm office and can't remember what lie I answered to most of her questions.

I wasn't up for that today.

I didn't think I was ever gonna be up to that any day. Never talked to so many adults in my whole life. It was getting right down to my last nerve.

Hell, I didn't have any nerves left.

So I did what my mom asked me not to do. I took the easy way out and asked Coco to do me a favor.

She came to the door in a star-burst caftan, her hair tied up in braids and a cup of coffee in her hand. "Hey, kid."

I carried Feather in, strapped in her carrier. Anybody would have wanted to keep her, dressed up cute in her pink teddy bear snowsuit.

Coco took the carrier from me and smiled.

All of a sudden my backpack is feeling heavy and it's all I can do not to fall on my knees to the soft carpet.

Coco says, "Running late? You need I should keep the little mouse pie?"

"Yeah, could you? I mean I wouldn't ask if the morning wasn't already shot, and my mom hadn't left about five this morning with every camera she had in the world to get some sunrise shots of the city."

"Hmmm." Coco hums.

"And she hasn't got back yet—Feather puking and it taking forever to get her to take a bottle."

I must have looked whacked 'cause Coco started unbuckling Feather while I held her coffee.

"Go to school, Bobby. I got her."

I could've cried and hugged Coco all at the same time but I just leaned over, kissed Feather, and told Coco I'd see her after school and what channel the purple dinosaur was on. She looked at me like I was crazy.

I should have hung with the first idea. Should have called off school and watched the big lizard with the kid all day.

then

J. L. RUNS TO THE DOOR to make sure what we hear out in the hall isn't going to get us kicked out of school for three days.

It's just some kid late for class.

And I don't even want to ask J. L. how he'd gotten the keys to Nelson's room. It's never good to know too much about what J. L. has in the back of his head. But it's cool 'cause it's usually kickin'.

Something stupid.

Something dumb.

Always funny.

Today we're turning everything in Nelson's room upside down. Desks, chairs, posters, garbage cans, whatever.

Just about the time we get to the desks, J. L. starts laughing and can't stop. *He's laughing so hard you can hear him in the hall,* I thought.

"Shut up, man. You're gonna get us busted."

J. L. pulls on his baseball cap and keeps laughing.

"Man, this is so stupid—what we're doing. It's so stupid I can't help it. . . ."

Then he starts laughing so hard he ends up on the floor.

I look at him curled up on the floor, gasping, then I look around the room and start laughing too. This is about the dumbest thing we ever did. But it feels good after the last couple of months with everything being so heavy with Nia and all.

We get out without getting caught, lock the room up, and push the extra set of keys back underneath the door. We walk to the third floor, get chips out of the machine, and head back to study group.

Never get to see how Nelson looks or how everybody laughs when they see the room 'cause five minutes after we're sitting back in group, the teacher gives me a note to say I'm excused.

Nia got real sick and was rushed to the hospital. And when I think the kid is here already, I remember she's only a few months pregnant.

I sit on the subway a few minutes later thinking, yeah, life is stupid.

Nia's sleeping when I get to the hospital.

I sit at the foot of her bed and rub her feet 'cause I know the only thing she likes more is having her back massaged. But I can't do that now.

The white sheet is curving around her stomach and I don't notice at first that the sheet is moving a little. I figure she's waking up, but when it does it again and her eyes are still closed, I know.

It's like a dream when I move my hands from her feet, up her legs and hips to her belly, and it kicks me.

I put my head on her stomach and it's like I'm stoned, and don't wake up till the nurse comes in to take Nia's temperature. I leave Nia sleeping.

Don't remember anything except how I walked about fifty blocks and it only seemed to take a few minutes to get home.

now

I LEAVE COCO'S APARTMENT and think how easy it would be if every morning fifty steps would get Feather to her baby-sitter.

Hell, that's living in a dream.

But all of a sudden I have time that I don't usually have.

No school for about an hour and a half.

And there's that thing I haven't done in a long time. Forgot that it used to juice me to do it, and now I need to do it, like yesterday.

I run back upstairs and put about four cans in my backpack before I go to Mineo's for a coffee and some kind of donut so full of sugar it almost blows my head off.

I'm feeling good.

Haven't felt this let loose in a while, and I almost can't stand it. Found this great wall a few weeks ago off the Ave. And it's time to do some tagging.

I cut through the parking lot and through the playground, an alley, and over and down a wall to get where I need to be. Perfect.

Everything is clean brown brick, and off in the shadows of some brownstones.

Where the hell did this wall come from anyway? It's just standing here in the middle of the city, not connected to anything or holding anything up. It's just been waiting for me.

I sit down against it. Feel the bricks and let the cool settle in me. I'm feeling colors and seeing things now that I'm against the wall.

There's flashes of me and K-Boy climbing up a fire escape and tying our kites to a clothesline and watching them all day.

After that, me and J. L. are at the Museum of Natural History in the shadows, looking at million-year-old rocks, and blowing bubbles on the front stairs.

Then I'm in Jamaica on a beach with my brothers burying me in the sand. My mom's snapping pictures of us while Fred keeps worrying that they'll get sand in my eyes.

In a few minutes my face is wet.

Tears are still pouring out when I start spraying the clean brick.

The tears are still coming when I start from the beginning and go to now.

I'm always the pale ghost boy between everybody. Floating in and out of the paintings. One minute I'm just getting J. L.'s face right.

I'm the pale white ghost boy beside the brown girl who is always looking away. Sometimes in the picture, my brothers show up, make themselves known, then leave the painting again.

Like in real life.

Finally it's just me and the thing in the baby carrier who doesn't have a face for a long time. There are bottles and boxes of diapers, hospitals, and social workers. There's the baby with no face and the ghost boy at the courts.

Then they're at the arcade and the bodega by K-Boy's house. The carrier sails through the painting, following the ghost boy. Pretty soon he's going to have to look inside the carrier and make up a face for the kid if it's gonna be following him all over the damned place anyway.

He's going to have to see it.

I spray black.

Then red, mixed with some blue.

The boy's got to be paler. But no, maybe just some green all around him. Maybe just some more green.

I'm losing wall now.

It's all got to come to an end soon. I'm going to have to find the kid's face. It's going to be hard now 'cause I'm out of breath and running out of color in the cans.

I'm almost empty.

But I got to find the baby's face.

And when I feel a hand on my shoulder, at first I think it's some kind of savior coming along to help me out. Help me find it's face.

Then I notice it's kind of dark and it isn't just dark from the building's shadows.

I've been here all day. Way past school, and near the night.

I get about two seconds of relief until the savior turns out to have a uniform and a gun, and I'm sitting in the back of the radio car all the way to the station.

part III

then

SO HERE'S A GOOD DAY.

We'll call it a fairy tale day.

Once upon a time, really right now, there was this hero (I always wanted to be one) who lived in the city. He was born in the city, loved the city, and never ever wanted to be anywhere else but the city.

He loved the feel of it. The way you got juiced when you walked down the sidewalk and everybody was out.

He loved the smell of it. Pizza on one corner, falafel and French pastries on the next. Standing in front of the Chinese restaurant, wondering if you want soup or if you should jump a train to that Jamaican place that K-Boy got kicked out of.

He loved the sounds that woke him in the morning and put him to sleep at night. And when he left the city and the noise to go someplace else—another country or town—he missed it.

Couldn't sleep without the ambulance noises and people calling to each other in the street who are just getting back from the clubs.

He couldn't help but get used to the delivery trucks that pulled up early for the restaurants in the neighborhood and the jackhammers and horns. He loved the sounds the kids made running to the subway, and cabs blowing by and screeching to a stop.

Now, 'cause this is a fairy tale, it's important to have some sort of monster, but I've decided not to include him in the story. Decided that because this was a perfect day, we didn't need him along to screw up the magical kingdom and run crazy through the streets, breathing fire and knocking down pizza joints and hot dog stands.

Whatever the monster is, it has to understand that the kid has got friends who hang out with him and usually got his back, and some days it just ain't worth it.

I mean even in a fairy tale the friends could be asses and stuff, give the hero a hard time when he gets stupid or something, but they're there. When everything gets real hard. Right there.

Now. The damsel.

Definitely in distress.

Sitting in a castle in Chelsea.

The hero is there to rescue her from her royal relatives who aren't evil, but lately have been trying to do a close imitation of it.

No white horse here.

Got a pass for the subway though.

The hero is buzzed up to the castle with his buddies waiting outside. The damsel's parents are at friends' having brunch and she's all alone. No mama dragon at the gate. No three deeds to do in order to open it up.

The damsel is all in black, dark glasses, and a smile 'cause she doesn't have to stay in her royal bedchambers anymore. The royal doctors just said not too much stress and watch the blood pressure.

The hero rides down the elevator with the damsel to meet his buddies on the street to go into the city kingdom and have the best time.

They go to the magical forest and watch the skaters, skateboarders, and other subjects laughing, talking, reading, eating, kissing, hugging, screaming. It's perfect that the magical forest runs right through the kingdom.

There's even a castle in the magical forest. They sit around the castle, eating popcorn, soda, and franks. The hero is happy with the damsel, who glows when the sun hits her curly hair and smiling face.

The buddies spend most of the time cracking on people and laughing at just about everything that moves. They each run around the magical forest, getting different foods for the damsel.

One even brings back a rock he swears looks like the super in his building.

He gives it to the damsel, saying, "Hey, girl, it's not Elvis, but you could keep it on top of some papers and think of my super."

The damsel says, "I don't know your super."

"So?"

"Shouldn't you keep it?"

"I don't want it."

The damsel eats another pretzel and laughs, "But it looks like your super."

The running buddy says, "Yeah, but I don't like our super."

So the damsel says, "We shouldn't be taking rocks out of the park anyway," and throws it across the grass into the trees. I forgot that the damsel has some arm.

The damsel sits back down and leans against

the hero. She's asleep in one minute. The hero covers her with his jacket.

And because this is a fairy tale, the hero and his running buddies lay back and talk about battles that they've won and places that they've seen.

There have been a lot of dragons.

More damsels for some than others.

They swam a lot of moats and ate many feasts. And mostly they've all done it together, 'cause a long time ago in the kingdom they became blood brothers, and that's what blood brothers do. Especially in a big kingdom like this one, on a good day that could be like a fairy tale.

now

I GOTTA CATCH A BREAK.

The cop who brings me in is on the phone, and looking through some file like she's got nothing to do but slowly look through paper.

We walk up tiled stairs past gray walls to a squad room.

She points to a chair and says, "Sit, kid."

I sit.

And when I look at the clock over the window facing a brick wall, I feel my stomach turning over. 7:30 P.M. Coco must be buggin' with my mom beside her, burning up every phone on the island.

By now my dad—who always thinks that way anyway—is imagining me cold in a Dumpster. It started as a real bad dream, but it's turning into a freakin' nightmare.

Then somebody is talking about night court and putting me in a holding cell till they get a hold of a parent.

All I'm thinking about in the gray cell, nasty 'cause I can tell somebody was sick a minute ago, is my baby. And how if I'm lucky I won't be murdered by her grandma if I get out of here in maybe—ever.

On the other side of things, I'm pretty scared about being dragged out of the station and being treated like I had been doing something dangerous and insane.

Doesn't Five-0 have anything to do besides bust underage artists? I want to ask, but I'm not talking 'cause that's what everybody says you should do.

Anyway, the cops can't do anything as bad to me as my mom can, and she never has to put a hand on me. All she has to do is walk around with a mom badge and her arms folded up serious tight in front of her.

Busted.

Mom lives by the rules and doesn't take bullshit—which is what skipping school, getting arrested for street art, and leaving Feather with Coco is.

Since both of Mom's parents were serious alcoholics, she can't take the crazy stuff. So we were dragged to meetings in church basements and school cafeterias. I guess she wanted to be ready when me and my brothers were on the street with forties in paper bags.

My one phone call is to my dad. I know he'll be in the restaurant, and he won't be nasty mad like my mom probably will. At least I think he won't.

8:45 P.M.

It's been fourteen hours since I dropped my baby off at Coco's house and I stepped into this. So I'm waiting for whoever to come get me so I can see just how big everything's been nuked.

He doesn't say anything to me in the station, but when we get into the cab he says, "Have you eaten?"

"No," I say, and try to look real interested in the raindrops on the taxi window.

"Do we need to stop by someplace and pick up takeout?"

"I'm not hungry, Dad," I whine.

"When was the last time you ate, anyway?" he says, looking real concerned, like he just picked me up from a hospital 'cause I passed out from lack of lunch, instead of the police station.

It's the way he deals.

Mom says if they could have just eaten the food he cooked twenty-four seven, and not had to deal with each other any other way, they'd still be married.

Whatever.

It's raining hard now.

"You left a mess at home, Bobby."

I feel like I'm going to throw up, again.

"You didn't call the sitter in Brooklyn to tell her you weren't going to show, so she got nervous. I guess there's about twenty messages from her."

"God."

"And since Coco couldn't get you on your cell . . . You know I got it for you so anyone who had the baby could stay in touch with you."

"I know, Dad. I know. I just didn't think about it being off."

He looks sad for me, but I must have been hallucinating 'cause the next second he's saying, "You seriously messed it up today. Coco couldn't get your mom, and I was out of the restaurant most of the day. She was on the verge of calling the cops."

"Shit," I say, then sink down lower in the seat

when I can feel my dad's eyes shooting holes through me in the dark taxi. "Sorry."

"There's going to be a whole lot of apologizing going on tonight, kid."

"Yeah, I guess so. All I want now is to go home, curl up in my bed, and sleep for two days."

Fred turns away from me.

"There'll be no sleep for you. There's ten pounds of I need my daddy, a pissed-off mother, and a disappointed neighbor waiting at home. You ready to deal?"

I say, "I guess," and sink farther into the seat.

My dad's shoulders come to the same part of the seat as mine, but I got longer legs. His face is kind and he's got laugh lines that don't crinkle like they used to. I guess I've taken a lot of his smile away.

And right now, besides a gurgling stomach and the look I know my mom is going to give me along with the hell, I feel worse because I'm taking my dad's smile and probably some more things he'll never talk about.

The taxi pulls up to the apartment. I look up to the third-floor window and see my mom's outline in the window. She's holding Feather.

My dad doesn't go in with me.

I think about how Feather is probably asleep

and will wake back up in two hours, and how she loves to be held. I climb the stairs and think about holding her, or maybe I'm really thinking about just holding on to her.

then

K-Boy STARTS LAUGHING in his sleep, then almost kicks himself awake. Something in his dreams is so funny he even shakes his head from side to side and acts like he's about to hold on to his stomach.

He's always laughed in his sleep, where J. L. doesn't move at all. He's in the same place from the time he goes to sleep till he wakes up in the morning.

I know how they sleep 'cause we used to nap together at preschool. We got in trouble more than we slept. Everybody is sleeping now, though.

We'd all stayed up late, first hangin' out at Mineo's till he'd kicked us out and told us to find a home or something. Then we'd gone up on the roof of K-Boy's building to play some new CDs he'd just got, till one of his neighbors started screaming that she was gonna call a cop if we didn't turn it down.

We didn't, till she came up to the roof.

She was seriously scary, so we left to hang out at my house 'cause my mom was gone for the night. We could eat most of the stuff in the icebox, then order Thai food if we were still hungry.

I still felt full and had slept like a pig when I finally did sleep, and now the phone's ringing.

"Hello," I say, and knock K-Boy's foot out of the way so I can get a bottle of water that rolled under my bed.

Nia's sleepy voice is on the other end.

"It's me. What did you do last night?"

"Hung with K-Boy and J. L."

She starts to eat something while she's talking. Then she burps real loud.

"Jeez, Nia. Did you get any on you?"

"Yeah, I did. If you were big as a house and had something living inside you, you'd burp out of control and make other disgusting noises too."

"Thanks for sharing that with me."

"I'd like to really share the whole damned

experience with you. How about the swollen ankles, or the aching back?"

"No, thanks."

She's getting started, I can tell, 'cause she takes a deep breath.

"How about the hemorrhoids or the constant peeing? How about how normal smells can make you sick or the way I can fall asleep in the middle of a sentence?"

I say, "Naw, that's okay." But I know it's not a joke anymore 'cause I can hear her voice getting high. It's like I can almost see her jangling the phone cord and shaking her leg.

I leave my room and go out in the hall. By the time I'm leaning against the wall outside of my mom's bedroom, Nia's crying. She does it so much now, but I'm still not used to it.

I whisper, "Sorry, Nia. I'm sorry everything is so messed up. I didn't mean for this to happen."

"Neither did I."

"I know it was my fault."

Nothing.

"I can 'fess to it. I was stupid."

I start to think that she's hung up the phone. I hear J. L. and K-Boy waking up in my room. My stereo comes on too loud for ten o'clock on a Sunday morning.

"Turn it down, man," I holler out to whoever turned it on in the first place. They turn it down.

"Nia."

Nothing.

"Nia."

Her voice is soft and low. "My parents are talking about sending me to my grandma's house in Georgia. They say I wouldn't be under so much stress there."

I want to cry. I want to cry a whole lot these days, and sometimes I do, and this makes me crazy.

"The doctor says my blood pressure is still too high. School and everything. They're talking about a tutor."

"In New York or Georgia?"

"Wherever, Bobby."

K-Boy must have seen someone out on the street 'cause I hear the window going up and him laughing and calling to somebody downstairs.

Nothing's changed and everything has. Whoever K-Boy called out to is doing the same ole same ole. I hear J. L. up, complaining about what's for breakfast. But Nia is talking about going. And even if she's not going, she's talking about it all being different.

"Bobby."

"Yeah."

"Do you want me to go?"

The music is getting loud slowly. K-Boy takes off the rap he started with and puts on some techno. I feel better when I say to Nia, "Don't go, okay? Don't leave."

She says, "Can we go out for pizza later? You can have anchovies on yours if you want."

"Cool with me."

"Cool with me too, Bobby. I'll see you later."

I walk into the kitchen to make breakfast, and even though nothing's changed yet, I miss her already.

now

HER EYES ARE THE CLEAREST EYES I've ever seen.

Sometimes she looks at me like she knows me. Like she's known me forever, and everything I ever thought, too. It's scary how she looks at me.

And she's so new. Been on the planet for only a few months. I been thinking about it a whole lot lately. I feel old.

I feel old when I wake up at three thirty in the morning and change her diaper, then change it again when she pees right after I put her sleeper back on.

I feel old when I stroll her into Mineo's, park her by my table while I eat a few slices and catch up on the comics I haven't read in weeks.

I really feel old when I'm holding her on the subway and some lady tells me what a good brother I am and how I'm so good with her. I feel stooped over then. You'd think I'd feel young.

For that one time on the way home I could pretend my baby is my sister. I could smile at the lady and say:

"Yeah, she's easy to deal with, my sister."

"She looks just like me and my brothers."

"I like to help my mom with her."

Even if I'm feeling old when this stuff happens I just change her diaper, put my food down and hold her when she cries, and tell the woman on the train that she's mine.

Afterward I always kiss her, my baby, and look into her clear eyes that know everything about me, and want me to be her daddy anyway.

then

"YOU GONNA DANCE, Bobby?"

"Yeah, in a minute."

My head's hurting. Never got a damned headache from music before. Too, too loud. The music is making the walls jump. I guess it's a good party.

Jess's parents are out of town for the weekend and most of the school is here. Actually I see more people at this party than I ever see at school.

Nia leans down and hollers in my ear.

"Now, Bobby?"

It's cool, I think, that she still feels like she wants to dance. She looks good dancing, even though she's really far along. She's been dancing with everybody.

Her and K-Boy haven't sat down all night.

Some girl trips over my feet and falls onto the couch beside me, spilling her diet soda all over my shirt. I don't think I've ever come home from a party without food or drink on me somewhere.

But that's okay.

I watch everybody dancing, laughing, talking, and stuffing chips in their faces. I'm feeling like an alien. And it goes way past me feeling like I don't belong here. I feel like I don't even know who all these people are or where they came from, and I've known most of them all my life.

Then Nia grabs my hands and we're dancing in the crowd. Somebody knocks over one of Mrs. Halem's vases and is trying to hide it behind a big-ass plant in the kitchen.

No way would I have even half these people in our apartment, but Jess isn't sweatin' it. She's over in the corner shaking her head at something "Moss" Green and J. L. are saying. Then she shrugs and goes off to dance with one of her friends who looks like she's had too much party.

She waves to Nia and screams over the music, "Haven't been this many people in the place since my Bat Mitzvah. Less fights, too."

Nia starts giggling and yells back, "Definitely less fights."

Then to me, "Two of her uncles seriously threw down in the kitchen. Her aunt ended up throwing a punch bowl, and her mom got so upset she threw up on the caterer."

"Good time, huh?"

"Oh yeah, too bad you missed it."

Then Nia smiles and I remember why I think of her all the time.

We slow dance even though the music is techno, rap, then techno again. She looks tired now, and dancing any faster would probably knock her out.

I take her hand and pull her toward the door. The smoke's starting to get to me. We walk down the hall toward the stairs. One of Jess's neighbors gets off the elevator, pulls a grocery cart behind him, stops and listens to the party. He shoots me and Nia a nasty look, and then goes into his apartment.

It echoes when I close the door, and we sit on the tiled green stairs. Nia leans against me, and for a minute I think she's asleep. She starts to breathe in and out in time with me. She's been so quiet she scares me when she says, "So what are we gonna do, Bobby?"

"About what?"

She puts my hand on her stomach and the

baby kicks. Her question probably scared it, too.

I can't answer, 'cause I really don't know what we're going to do. I'm thinking about what's going to happen, but I don't know what to feel.

I can't imagine a real baby.

Can't imagine going over to Nia's parent's house and holding the baby while they look at me and make me sweat and my stomach hurt. As it is, I make sure they aren't home when I see Nia now.

Can't imagine changing diapers or even feeding a baby 'cause I never had before. I'm the youngest in my family. People fed and put diapers on me.

I say, "We'll be okay. Our parents are gonna help."

"Yeah, I know—but in the end it's all up to us."

"I guess it's always been up to us."

She leans against me again. "I don't want to do it."

"Do what, Nia?"

"I don't want to be anybody's mother. I'm not done with being a kid myself. I'm way too young and so are you."

"No choice now."

She gets up and walks toward the door.

"My mom talked about adoption, but I don't

know if that would make me bug. I mean the idea that I could be passing my own kid every day and not know it. And what about college? A baby, then?"

I get up and wrap my arms around her 'cause we'd made the decision by waiting so long. We didn't want to face it, but now it's all in our face. Nothing to do but get on with it 'cause it's happening no matter how freaked out we get.

Nia tells everybody that they have to take her like she is.

I always have.

I still do.

Nia opens the door, but backs up when cigarette smoke hits her in the face. The party's getting louder.

She walks back over to me. "Wanna dance, Bobby?"

I do.

now

My brother Paul holds Feather, and she smiles drooly baby gums at him while her arms jerk up and down. He's good with her.

He's good with everybody.

His two kids, Nick and Nora (he got their names from his favorite movie characters), crawl all over the floor and Mary. Fred is in the kitchen making fajitas, and if I close my eyes I can remember that this was the way it used to be.

Paul remembers too, 'cause he looks over at me and smiles. I like having him here. All of a sudden I don't feel so alone.

"Cute kid," he says, then changes holding arms. Feather keeps making happy baby noises. And when Nick and Nora run over to their dad, they start to kiss her all over her face and head. Most times she'd scream. Now she gurgles and jumps.

"Yeah, she's pretty cute."

"Does she give you much trouble?"

I pull at Feather's feet, bare for once, even though mom keeps eyeing her socks on the couch, from across the room.

"Normal stuff. Too much baby sh—err crap, sleepless nights, seriously cranky me. . . ."

Paul watches Nick and Nora sing a song to Feather.

"That's it in the beginning. It ain't pretty."

"You tellin' me?"

"Yeah, well I guess you know, Bobby. It gets better, though. I mean the crawling and first steps make you so happy. Then it freaks you 'cause you know they're slowly getting away from you and heading for the world."

All I can do is shrug to that, 'cause the thought had crossed my mind at two in the morning once how I was going to be a lot happier helping this kid with homework than I was changing a bad case of formula diarrhea.

Nora crawls in my lap and smiles up at me. She looks like Paul. Tall, skinny, black eyes, and always smiling. I can't tell who Nick looks like 'cause he hasn't sat still since he got here.

Mom says it's too much sugar.

Paul says it was him sitting too long in the car.

I say the boy hasn't ever sat still in his whole life, so why are they making excuses for it now?

I like Nick, though, 'cause he's harder to deal with. Nora is easy to like, but I love them both.

Nick is the six-year-old from hell. The good kind of hell, where they play music all day long and get on the nerves of everybody that was ever born, but it's still a good time.

"What's up, Nick?"

He smiles, pinches Nora—she ignores him—and tells me he helped his dad fix the sink a couple days ago.

"How'd that go for you?"

"It was okay till Daddy told me too late not to pour the orange juice down the sink."

Paul's frowning.

"I had the pipes out. Orange juice burns when it gets in your eyes, and besides, I almost drowned."

Dad starts laughing from the kitchen. Mary thinks it's pretty funny too, and I figure they're really laughing so hard 'cause they know Nick won't be living with either of them, so everything he does makes them happy.

Paul looks at them, shakes his head, and says, "It's the revenge theory. They're laughing at me for everything I ever did to them when I was a kid."

"I'm toast then." I look over at Feather who looks like she'll laugh any minute. I know I'm toast. It's been a hell of a year so far for Mary and Fred thanks to me.

Paul laughs, "Feeling doomed?"

"Oh yeah."

"It's a good doomed. Even though I still think you're too young."

"I hear that."

Paul looks sorry for me. He's the only one that didn't say the obvious when he found out I'd gotten Nia pregnant. I felt better telling him than anybody. He was the one person who I knew would say what I needed to hear. I don't remember the exact words, but I felt good when he said them.

"Want to go for a walk, Bobby?"

I nod and take Feather from him to start getting her ready, but Mary comes over and takes her from me.

"Your dad and I will keep all the kids. You two go off and hang out for the rest of the afternoon."

I must look like I'm in shock 'cause Mom

never has said or done that for me since Feather's been here. But now she's looking at me like I'm a baby that just walked across the room for the first time.

Maybe I just did.

I'm laughing so hard at my brother telling me about his neighbors in the little town in Ohio he lives in. He lives near Lake Erie in a place called Heaven. He moved there to be close to his kids after he divorced his wife, Melanie.

He says, "I never thought I could live in a small town."

We get pretzels on the corner and walk toward the movie theater.

"I always dreamed of living in a small town. Green grass, creeks, cows. That all seems perfect. Especially because me and Feather are going back to Brooklyn to live with Dad. I guess it's his turn now. Anyway, I miss the old neighborhood."

"What happened? Why are you going back to Brooklyn?"

"There was a thing. I blew off school and things got stupid. Postal baby-sitter, cops, etcetera, etcetera. Mary's out of town too much and Fred thinks I need more prison guard time.

You know, the kid with the baby needs to be treated like one."

We sit down on the benches in the rec center playground, finish our pretzels, and watch the kids.

Just sittin' quiet.

Finally Paul says, "What about college for next year? What's the good of you being able to graduate when you're sixteen if you're not going to college?"

"I figure I'd just get a Mcjob for a year and try to save some money."

"You'd get to spend more time with Feather."

I look at Paul and then at the running, screaming kids jumping up and down on the playground. Feather will be them one day, and I'll be one of the scared, happy, mad, yelling, smiling parents who sit on the benches and watch. Just watch it all happen.

I say it like I've known it forever, only now it's so clear and I can say it: "I've never been closer to or loved anybody more than I love Feather."

Paul throws a ball back to a group of kids over by the slide and says, "I know that, kid. I know that."

then

The office has babies, kids, and smiling adults hugging and happy all over the walls. I'm holding Nia's hand. Her back's been aching all day, and even me trying to bribe her with pizza, no anchovies, only makes her moan.

Her mom and my dad are sitting behind us. I don't want to turn around and see Fred's face. The last time I looked at him in the cab, he looked a little wigged.

Mrs. Wilkins sometimes leans forward and rubs Nia on the shoulders. I'm thinking it's not really making Nia feel any better. Every time her mom touches her she jumps like she's being hit.

But it's just a reflex.

• • •

If we give our baby up, we could get on with it. Go to college. Go on spring break. Go to parties. Come home on breaks with dirty laundry like my brothers did, and eat everything in the cabinets and fridge.

We could hate our roommates, their music, and their friends. Lie to our parents about our midterm grades and how when they called late on a Tuesday we were at the library.

I want to stay up all night and meet so many people I forget their names. And I want to meet people I might get to know forever.

I don't want to be here.

I don't want to be at home.

I know I should be listening to everything the social worker (fifth one we've talked to—I forget her name) is saying, but I'm not. I figure if I block it all out I won't have to think about it.

She's talking about parental rights.

Waiting periods.

Counseling during the waiting period.

Open adoption.

And all I want to do is paint on the walls. Paint me running through the city and over the bridge.

I want to spray black, greens, and reds all over this office and cover the smiling faces of the kids and the grown-ups.

What the hell are they smiling for?

Do they know some secret nobody's told me or Nia? 'Cause we didn't want a baby anyway, and I can't believe we'll be smiling in some damned picture after we do the right thing.

It's the right thing. Everybody says so, and I want to believe the shit everybody says. I want to believe it's unselfish. I want to believe none of this is supposed to be about me.

Then the social worker says, "Now, do you have any questions?"

Nia asks, "Can we meet them? The people who are going to get the baby. . . ."

"Well that goes back to whether you are going to have a traditional adoption or an open one.

"Now . . ." Then she goes on.

This woman is nice and looks us in the face to see if we're getting any of it. Mostly we're not, but she keeps on going.

Nia's tired and sore.

I'm freakin' and in shock when everybody says I should be relieved and throwing a party. The hard part is that they're right and I should be happy. Right?

In a few minutes we're all standing out in the hall. Nia and me lean against the wall and look straight ahead at a billboard that talks about reproductive responsibility.

There's a girl, about thirteen, holding a baby.

We keep leaning against the wall and don't talk to our parents who are shaking the social worker's hand and telling her that they have to make calls and whatever.

I take out some bubble gum and hand Nia a piece.

We're still blowing bubbles when we walk out of the office hand in hand, then get into separate taxis with our parents and head to different parts of the city.

now

I THINK SHE KNOWS we're someplace else.

She just fell asleep on my stomach after being wide-eyed and whining all night long. I feel sorry for her. But it's good to be back in the old hood.

Dad's been poking his head in the room all night, asking if everything is okay and did I need him to take her. The first time he asked I wanted to say, "Take her where?"

But I just shake my head. He leaves my door open like he wants to hear her if she cries.

Mom always shut hers tight. She says so she wouldn't be tempted to do what most grandmothers would do. Take over.

There still are a whole bunch of times I want

her to take over, even more than I feel right about having. But she never does.

She only ever changed, fed, or rocked Feather to sleep when I didn't need her help. But she warned me. She said I was the parent. She was only the grandparent.

"It's your world, kid," she said a couple days after Feather was born.

After the last of our things were moved into Dad's apartment, she got back into her Jeep and sat there without turning the ignition. I stood on the stoop with Feather, wondering what was wrong.

Hell, she was always in a hurry to be anyplace but where she was. So I walked over to the Jeep and knocked on the window on the passenger side.

She was crying.

Damn, that scared me. I held on to Feather real hard then, and only loosened up when she squeaked.

"Haven't ever seen you cry before, Mom."

Even though she had dark glasses and a hat on, I knew it.

"Check me out, kid, 'cause you won't be seeing me do it again anytime soon. That crying shit is what your old man does."

"Yeah," I say. "He's pretty good at it."

"Yep, that's him, cooking and crying. He always was too sensitive."

She's smiling though.

"And that's why I know you two are going to be fine with him. He'll baby both of you."

"Not like you, huh?"

She leans back, then starts the car up.

"No, not like me, and that's a good thing. I don't think you and your brothers could have stood *two* parents like me."

I stand back and she rolls the window up, then blows two kisses and heads back home.

When I turn around, Dad is standing on the stoop with a baby quilt. "Isn't it getting too chilly out here for the baby?"

And a cup of coffee for me.

We walk back to the apartment and I fall asleep with Feather asleep on me surrounded by our boxes.

I wake up to different neighborhood sounds, but it all comes back. It's five thirty in the morning and I'm walking Feather around, looking out the windows of the apartment.

I put on coffee for Dad and open boxes that I don't want to think about unpacking. No hurry,

Fred says. He knows how busy I am with the last of school and the baby.

Whenever will be okay.

I kiss the top of Feather's curly head and hold her close. She shivers a little, so I grab my Mets sweatshirt and wrap her in it.

She yawns and looks at me like she's going to ask me something, and I'll be damned if she doesn't look just like Nia.

She looks at me with those eyes that know me.

I know then that even when everything's changing, Feather's not gonna mind as long as she's with me.

then

NIA SAYS SHE'S BEEN HAVING DREAMS that she's in a nest. When my mom says from her darkroom—which used to be a walk-in closet—"That makes sense. You know, babies and nesting," Nia leans back on the pillows she's propped up behind her on the floor and says, "No, it's not like that. It was a bad dream 'cause I wasn't a bird. I was this small person in a nasty bird's nest with all kinds of old pieces of clothes and bones. . . ."

"Jeez," J. L. says, then sucks down the gallon of soda he always has with him.

K-Boy stares at Nia. "So what did you do when the bird tried to feed you some already chewed-on worms?"

Nia rolls her eyes at him. "You always know exactly what to say that's going to make me barf."

K-Boy puts his feet on the back of Nia's pillow until she twists around and knocks them off. "Could you be more annoying, or are you waiting for somebody to knock you down before you do it again?"

"Waiting."

"Yeah, okay." Nia starts to rub her lower back. It's eight months now. She must be tired of being pregnant. Anyway, in a month it'll all be over. We decided the other day, it would all be over.

Nia cried.

I cried.

My dad cried.

But we were the only ones. My mom and Nia's parents looked like they just got released from Oz, and not the one with the yellow brick road. I think Nia's dad took his first real breath since the first time he found out she was having a baby.

Her mom smiled at me—which freaked me out.

The baby was going to one of those happy, smiling people in the pictures. It would live in a house with a yard and a dog and a swing set. All the pictures had yards and dogs.

It would all be back the way it was before, in a month. Nothing would have changed. We'd leave school and keep on going.

No baby in a month.

now

FEATHER CRIED YESTERDAY when I left her at the sitter's. It's the first time she ever cried for me. I didn't know it till Jackie told me today, though.

"Look at the way she frowns up when you walk away. She did it when you left her yesterday, too."

"Really?"

"Oh yeah. What? Does that surprise you?" Jackie picks up a little girl who just started walking and was hanging on to her pants.

Feather's in her carrier, kicking and smiling now that I'm in her face. I lean close to her and smell her sweet baby head and kiss her cheeks.

Now it's hard to go. Now that she knows

when I'm not around it's so hard to go. And now I look at her and I see Nia. All the way through her I see Nia.

K-Boy waits across the street at the Laundromat. J. L. is spinning around in one of the dryers.

"Hey, man, what took you so long? J. L. got in the dryer when he thought he saw the principal crossing the street for a smoke."

I walk over to the dryer and stop it.

J. L. starts laughing while he's still inside. He's all tangled up in somebody's comforter.

"Crazy much, J. L.?"

He falls out of the dryer and folds the comforter and puts it on the big wooden table over by the vending machines.

"Naw, man. Just cold and tired of not falling down when I walk a straight line. What took you so long?"

"Uh, there's this thing called school. Leaving it before two thirty can get you busted to detention or worse; having to tell your dad he has to leave work to talk to the guidance counselor, again."

K-Boy eats popcorn and reads a fashion magazine, leaning against a washer.

"We gonna do this or what?" he says.

J. L. keeps looking at the dryer like he wants to get back in it.

K-Boy says, "Is this going to be a thing with you, man? I mean, you gonna be calling up your friends outside of laundries asking for change and spin time?"

J. L. grabs the magazine from K-Boy, and we all go out the back way through the alley. It's been our (and everybody else's that goes to our high school) getaway since, ever.

We head off through the city, feeling the way you feel when you just got out of something like the dentist or a test. We talk and eat junk all the way to Grand Central.

An hour later we're on a train headed out of the city. Heading out of the city to see Nia.

Feather has sweet sticky marks on her face where the baby who just learned to walk's been trying to share ice cream with her. Every time the little girl comes near her she kicks and shows her gums in a smile that's begging for more of what's on her face.

I scoop up the diaper bag, Mr. Moose, her favorite thing to gum on, and Feather and head out the door with Jackie reminding me Feather has a doctor appointment tomorrow. We walk out into the sun with kids running up and down the sidewalks.

Everybody's out.

It's April and summer doesn't feel like something so far away anymore. Feather sighs and blinks when a beam of sun hits her in the face.

Now we're only three blocks from Jackie's house. No subway to get her there. No getting up three hours before school starts.

Some kids my age are hanging around this arcade I've been wanting to check out, but haven't had the time, and probably won't ever have. They lean against the games and each other. I look at them and feel like I'm missing something.

Then I think—I got K-Boy and J. L. I mean not like before. But I still got them. It'll never be like before, but I still got 'em.

I get to our building and go up the elevator.

"We're home, baby."

She knows it 'cause all of a sudden she seriously needs a diaper change.

Dad's left a note on the fridge that I see when I go to make Feather a bottle:

FOOD IN THE FRIDGE. A LETTER FROM YOUR BROTHER.

I feed Feather and read my letter from Paul out loud. She relaxes in my arms, and after a few minutes the formula in her bottle isn't as important as sleeping is. I take her to our room and try to put her in her crib, but she isn't that sleepy.

She just looks pissed and dares me to put her down.

So I don't, and keep reading to her. When I'm done reading I sit holding her by the bedroom window and tell her what I did today. And just about the time her eyes close shut, I tell her about her mom.

then

I USED TO WATCH COMMERCIALS when I was little. I'd run in from the bedroom I shared with my brother Nick every time one came on.

I knew all the words to commercials for floor cleaner and cars, breakfast cereals and soda, fast food places and car batteries. I knew 'em all and used to sing commercials day in and out.

I'm singing a video rental commercial to Nia's stomach now. Since the baby won't be talking to me as it's growing up this has to be enough, even if it is just stupid commercial jingles.

Nia thinks it's cute, and looks at me like I'm a puppy, then curls up on the couch and goes to sleep. I sing a few more commercials to the baby, then get up to leave.

I'm still dodging her parents. I can't help it. K-Boy laughs at me about it, but he spends his time trying to feel superior. I got reason.

I touch Nia on the back before I head out the door, leaving her smiling in her sleep. I walk onto the street singing a shampoo commercial.

Nia

WHEN I WAS FIVE *I wanted to be a firefighter.
All my uniforms would have Nia on them, and I would
speed through the city in the lightning trucks. I wanted
the ladders to rise high into the sky and have me on them.
I wanted my hands to pull people from fires and disas-
ters. I wanted my arms to be the arms that carried out
babies and kids, safe. I wanted my feet to be the ones that
ran up endless flights of stairs and brought everybody
back alive.*

*But by the time I was ten I wanted to be a balloon-
ist, and just fly up high over everybody, and that's what
it feels like I'm doing now.*

*I'm flying up high over everybody; way over the city
and even myself. I'm flying over Bobby and my parents,*

and the park with all my friends in it. I guess this is what it must feel like to be dying.

All I want to do is lie here and sleep, even though I see the blood and it shouldn't be where it is. And it was just a minute ago Bobby was singing a shampoo commercial, but he's gone now.

But that's okay because all I want to do is fly.

now

I TELL FEATHER ABOUT HER MOM.

She never liked to wear shoes, but always had to, 'cause you do when you're surrounded by cement. She liked tacos better than anything, and always ate the extra sauce straight out of the packet.

She cheated at cards and didn't care who knew. Socks got on her nerves, and she had fifty pairs of sunglasses and seventy hats.

She got in fights at school when she saw somebody being mean to somebody else, even though she could be mean too and very funny.

While she was pregnant with you, fish made her sick, but she ate spicy food all the time.

And all she wanted to do while she was pregnant was swim, but she'd never learned how.

There's a picture of her right before you were born, with a big smiling face painted on her stomach. She liked to sit on the floor and hide under tables so she could eavesdrop.

You look just like her in baby pictures.

Feather stretches, yawns, then opens her eyes for a second before she snores once and goes back to sleep.

I tell her, I saw your mom today.

K-Boy told her jokes that she probably didn't hear, and J. L. played her his new CD and danced around her bed till one of the nurses came in and gave him a nasty look.

I told her what I was going to wear to graduation, and how you preferred the night to the day, liked ice cream already, and how Mr. Moose made you smile.

I asked her if she remembered how I put you on her stomach before they took her away from the city and away to the country for something called long-term care. I asked her if she was ever going to wake up, and if she really believed what the doctors said to her parents about brain damage.

I told her about you and how you were mine, not the smiling, happy people's baby; 'cause now that she was gone I wouldn't sign the papers.

I got tired after a while and J. L. went looking for food, then K-Boy went to sleep on the chair beside her bed, but I kept telling her about you, Feather.

The nurse came in and turned her over.

Another nurse came in and cleared her breathing tube.

But it didn't matter what was going on, baby; I kept telling her about you.

Damn right, I kept telling her about you.

then

I TRIED NOT TO RUN, but I did.

I tried not to cry, but when I looked down at my shirt it was soaked; with me wanting to believe it was sweat. By then, though my nose was running and I couldn't even see the faces of the people, I ran into the street.

And I must have been screaming. . . .

Must have looked crazy and desperate, but it was better for me to run all the way to the hospital from my mom's 'cause the note on the door said meet her there, something had happened to Nia.

The whacked part was I didn't start trying to make a deal with God till I was almost running through the doors. And when I see my mom's face I know I got to catch up.

So I start begging.

I say how it's supposed to work out 'cause we thought about it. We made a mistake but we aren't stupid. We were going to do the right thing.

Then I guess I start babbling about how Nia looks when she sleeps and how she smiles and eats and laughs, but I have to stop 'cause even though I don't think about God or go to church, maybe this isn't the way you make deals with him.

Maybe he doesn't listen if you scare everybody in the emergency room and hold on to your mom that tight while you're screaming and crying more than you ever have in your whole damned life.

Maybe if you'd said out loud how much you felt in the beginning you wouldn't have to look at her parents' faces when they walk out the automatic double doors.

And my mom's whispering in my ear, past the screaming, "Hold on, Bobby, hold on," like she did when I had poison ivy all over my body when I was nine and she held my hand while I cried on cool white sheets.

Hold on, Bobby. Hold on.

I want to tell Mr. Wilkins to hold on to his wife harder 'cause right in front of the doctors, nurses, me, and my parents she's starting to disappear.

In a minute, it's too late.

She's gone.

Just like that. No noise. Not a word.

She walks over to the window and looks out it like she's a tourist. She's seeing everything for the first time and she doesn't even know us.

She's holding Nia's favorite stuffed animal, and all I can think is she grabbed it to make Nia feel better, but when I look at her again, I change my mind.

It's for her.

We all sit at a round table, but none of us are knights.

My parents make soft sounds at Nia's parents and ask the doctor questions.

Nia's father nods his head at everybody and cries when the doctor closes his folder, pats him on the back, and leaves. Mrs. Wilkins holds hands with her husband, but I don't know how she keeps a grip, 'cause she's been invisible since the emergency room.

I can't ever be a knight or brave, so I ask nothing about brain death or eclampsia or why the girl who had a thousand pair of sunglasses and my baby inside her won't ever walk, talk, or smile again. And I have to say irreversible vegetative coma five times, like a tongue twister, to believe it.

And I feel like a three-year-old when I walk out the room between my parents while they hold my hands. Mr. Wilkins starts crying, then falls to his knees, and it's only then that Nia's mom comes back from the invisible place and rocks him in her arms.

I carry around a picture of me, Nia, K-Boy, and J. L. at the beach. A minute before the picture was taken by J. L.'s sister we were all out in the water, splashing around, having fun.

I had to fold the picture in half so it would fit in my wallet. I like the way Nia's laughing and the rest of us look pissed.

Nia's laughing 'cause just as the picture is snapped she tells us she's given all our clothes to some kids who said they needed them for Halloween.

It was July, but we believed her.

J. L.'s sister has the next picture of us running back to the water. It doesn't show our faces, only our backs while we chase her out into the white water.

I guess I think of it when I turn around in the waiting room and see the backs of both my buddies talking to my dad. But I know they won't be laughing like we did, or yelling "Get her" like we did.

But they're here, and she won't ever be running away from any of us again. In a few minutes, though, they're beside me and in the white light of the waiting room. I miss Nia for the first time, but feel her more than I ever did.

It wasn't fast or blurred. Didn't knock me out or make me fall against the wall.

She came to me slowly.

Somebody covered in hospital clothes head to foot pushed the incubator toward me down the longest hall I've ever been in.

My mom and dad talked over my shoulders, and Mr. and Mrs. Wilkins cried over by the nurses' station.

She came to me so slowly I felt like I was in a dream. Four steps away, three, then two . . .

Then she was all dark hair, hands in fists, Nia's nose and mouth. She came to me so slow, and it was just like somebody brushed the air with a feather.

I just came from the nursery.

Feather doesn't like being wrapped up in her blanket. She fights against the binding. I like that she does that. I like that the only thing that makes her not fight is me holding her in the rocking chair in the hospital family room.

It's been an hour since I did it.

The social worker tried about five minutes of reasoning. She kept tapping her pencil against her desk. I think she was saying the things she thought she should say.

"I know this is an emotional time for you, Bobby. I can't think what you must be going through. Nia's condition—have the doctors said anything else?"

I look at the smiling families on the wall.

"They keep saying 'persistent vegetative.' I hate when they say it, but there it is."

"Bobby, the baby . . ."

"Feather. Her name is Feather."

"We have to think in the end what's best for her. Are you ready for this? Do you know what raising a baby entails?"

I look at the adoption papers stacked in front of me, then fold them in half before I tear them.

"No, I don't know anything about raising a kid. I'm sixteen and none of those people on the wall look like the kind of family me and Feather's gonna be. But I'm doing it."

The social worker's forehead wrinkles up.

"You don't have to do it. This baby is wanted. There's a family that wants her. They're set up to take her and love her—"

"But *I* love her, and even though I'm not set up for her, she's mine. And I'm hers."

When I walk out of the office I think I see "Just Frank" standing at the end of the hall. And then I know I'm being a man, not just some kid who's upset and wants it his way.

I'm being a man.

Before all the papers turned into shreds, I talked to Nia's parents.

I talked; they listened.

They talked; I listened.

They cried.

I almost cried.

And when Mrs. Wilkens started telling me how much the baby looked like Nia and she's all they'll ever have of their daughter, I did start to cry. But I wiped my eyes real fast on the back of my sleeve 'cause I'm going to be this baby's daddy now.

I don't know any of the parent rules, but crying like a baby when you just decided to keep a baby probably shouldn't happen.

"We'll support you keeping the baby, Bobby,"

was all they said in the end. But when they looked at the baby through the nursery glass, it was like they were saying good-bye.

Soon Feather is home with me sleeping on my stomach.

Three days ago everything was different. She wasn't here and she was never going to be with me.

Now she's three days and nine hours old, won't sleep through the night, and my mom—her grandmother—only smiles at her when I'm not looking. But it's all okay 'cause I know now better than I ever did that I'm supposed to do this. I'm supposed to be her daddy and stay up all night if I have to. I'm supposed to suck it up and do all the right things if I can, even if I screw it up and have to do it over.

It's all right for now, 'cause for the first time I get to watch the coming of the soft morning light.

now

BABY, DO YOU WANT TO hear more about Heaven? Do you want to know more about the fields, and grass, and cows? Do you want to wonder what it would be like to have a deer wake you up by eating on a tree outside your window?

Do you want to know more about somewhere else that's not here?

"What you thinking about, Bobby?"

I jump 'cause I think it's the first time my dad has ever asked me this question. And, because it's the first time, I think I should come up with something good.

What to say?

I got a little time to think. Feather went down

for a nap a minute ago and won't wake up till her formula digests and she needs some more. For once I don't have anything to do and the sun is shining down Seventh Ave.

What to say?

Do I say I'm glad I'm back in Brooklyn and wanted more than anything for Feather to see more trees? Do I tell him I'm glad I'm back with him 'cause he puts the covers over me at night and kisses Feather all the time before he leaves the room?

Or do I tell him that I'm thinking I need something else 'cause of everything that's happened? Everything.

Do I tell him how my whole body hurt when I went to see Nia in the nursing home the other day? Do I describe how skinny she is and how soft her lips were when I kissed her good-bye?

Maybe I'll just tell him how I don't think I'll make it if I stay here. In this place. In this state.

Maybe I'll just tell him how I feel like I'm a baby with a baby most of the time. Just playing daddy until somebody comes over and says, "Hell, kid, time's up. No more of this daddy thing for you, and anyway you've been busted."

Maybe I'll tell him how all of a sudden the city just feels like it's too big and I've been having dreams that I leave Feather on the subway and can't get back inside the train fast enough to get her, and she disappears forever.

Maybe I should tell him all that and then he'll make me something good to eat and we'll turn on one of the sports channels and watch baseball all into the night.

Instead I say, "Paul says he loves Ohio and it's a good place to raise kids."

Dad goes over to the window and squints into the sun.

"Your brother might be right, Bobby, he just might be right."

And then me and Dad turn on the sports channel and talk about how we should have checked the Mets out more.

heaven

I WON'T TALK about the good-byes.

I won't talk about how for a month I went to every place in the city that I loved so much, so many times that K-Boy and J. L. thought I was whacked.

I won't say how much I'm going to miss everybody and how if it wasn't for Pennsylvania I'd be one hour from Brooklyn instead of eight and I'd have the best of all of it.

I won't say.

I won't talk about how, I woke up one night to my mom rocking Feather and telling her to mind me and take care of me.

I will talk about how, when I finally visited Paul in Heaven, Ohio, the town was out of some old postcard and Feather smiled at everybody when we walked down the main street.

I will talk about how the grass smelled and how the horses looked running in the fields outside of town. And how I decided the little apartment by the car repair shop with its big front window and bikers hanging around all day had to be ours.

I will talk about how I didn't know if it would all work out as me and Feather pulled out of New York on the bus, and waved to everybody we'd left behind.

I can talk about how it felt to be holding my baby in my arms on the long ride, getting off the bus when we had to and sleeping the rest of the time.

I can tell you how it feels sitting in the window with Feather pointing out the creek that rolls past our backyard. I can tell you how it is to feel as brand new as my daughter even though I don't know what comes next in this place called Heaven.

about the author

ANGELA JOHNSON received her first major liter-
ary prize in 1991 when her second book *When I
Am Old with You* was named a Coretta Scott King
Honor book. Since that time, Angela won two
Coretta Scott King Awards, for the novels *Heaven*
and *Toning the Sweep,* and a second Coretta Scott
King Honor for *The Other Side: Shorter Poems*. Her
most recent novel for Simon & Schuster is
Looking for Red. She lives in Kent, Ohio.

About the Author